W9-BMT-679

URSULA K. LE GUIN

TOM MOUSE

PICTURES BY JULIE DOWNING

ROARING BROOK PRESS
Brookfield, Connecticut

For India and Isabel from Ama
—U.K.L.

To Margaret and Nkrumah
—J.D.

A NEAL PORTER BOOK

Text copyright © 2002 by Ursula K. Le Guin
Illustration copyright © 2002 by Julie Downing

Published by Roaring Brook Press
A division of The Millbrook Press, 2 Old New Milford Road, Brookfield, Connecticut 06804

All rights reserved

Library of Congress Cataloging-in-Publication Data
Le Guin, Ursula K., 1929-
Tom Mouse / Ursula K. Le Guin ; pictures by Julie Downing.
p. cm.
"A Neal Porter book."
Summary: Tom Mouse hides on the train he has boarded for travel and adventure, but
an old woman finds and befriends him.
I. Mice—Juvenile fiction. [I.Mice—Fiction. 2. Railroads—Trains—Fiction. 3. Travel—Fiction.
4. Friendship—Fiction.] I. Downing, Julie, ill. II. Title.
PZ10.3.L529 To 2002 [E]—dc21 2001041893

ISBN 0-7613-1599-3 (trade)
0-7613-2663-4 (library binding)

Book design by Jennifer Browne
Printed in the United States of America

2 4 6 8 10 9 7 5 3 1
First edition

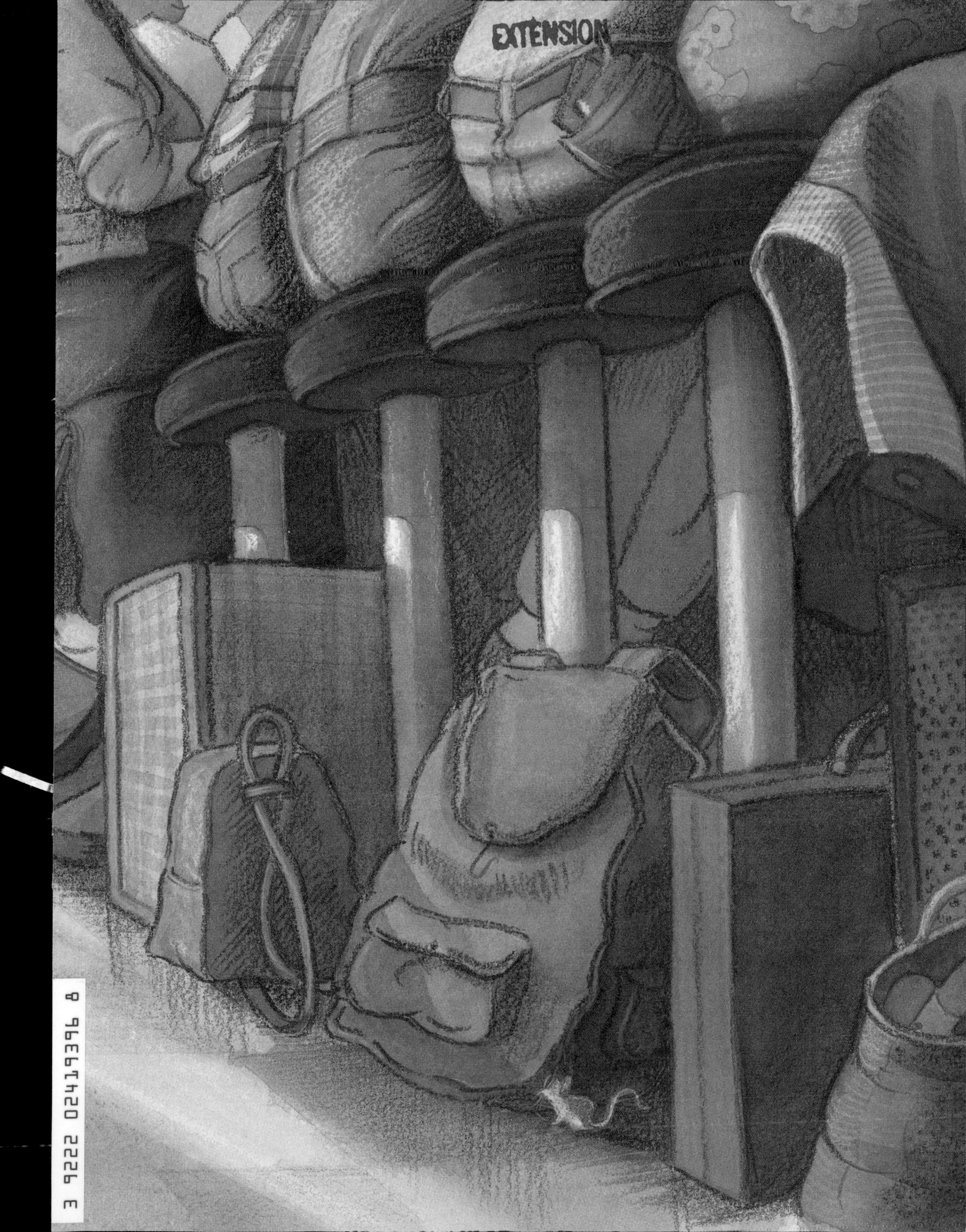

3 9222 02419396 8

He scurried across the platform and down onto the tracks and across them, trying to keep in shadows and under crossties. As he crossed one of the great steel tracks, it trembled, feeling the train coming a

TOM MOUSE GREW UP in a hole in the wall of the diner in the station. His family was content with their cozy nest and the doughnut crumbs and bits of bacon they picked up in the diner. But Tom watched the great trains come into the station and leave again, and he wished he could go with them.

An old hobo rat who rode the freight trains stopped off one day, and he talked to Tom. "All you have to do," he said, "is hop a ride on a boxcar, and you're off! From Chicago to San Francisco and back again, you're free as the wind, all alone and on your own!"

So Tom put a doughnut crumb and a bit of bacon in his cheek pocket, kissed his dear family good-bye, and set out to be free as the wind.

mile away. Tom crouched by the end of a crosstie. He looked down the track and thought, "San Francisco!" He looked up the track and thought, "Chicago!" The thunder of the train shook everything. The huge wheels came past, slowed down, and stopped.

Tom ran forward, climbed up a wheel, leaped to the step of an opening door, and quick as a wink he was in!

"Look for a boxcar," the hobo rat had told him, but Tom in his hurry hadn't looked at all. Now he crouched very small in a corner and wondered where he was. Feet were going by just the way they did in the diner and the station, feet in shoes, high heels, low heels, Mary Janes, and tennis shoes. This train was full of people, all putting their luggage onto racks and sitting in seats by big windows. Where could a mouse hide?

Before him were narrow, twisting stairs. No feet were going up and down them now. He skittered right up the stairs, and then along a narrow corridor, till he saw through an open door a room with nobody sitting in it. Just inside the door was a tall, thin closet all made of metal, with slots near the floor to let air inside. The car porter was coming down the corridor, his big, black, shiny shoes thumping up right behind Tom's tail. Tom squeezed through the air vent into the closet and crouched there in the dark, his heart pounding, his whiskers shivering.

"All aboard!" the conductor shouted outside the car.

"On my own and all alone!" Tom thought, and when the train gave a little jerk and slid forward, he nearly burst into tears.

After a long time he got up his courage and ventured out of the closet. He climbed up onto the seat, and onto the shelf under the window, and put his little paws on the glass. He gazed at the world. The beautiful hills and trees and clouds flew by. A herd of horses and a herd of cows flew by. A little town and a tall grain silo flew by. Everything flew by and was gone. "I'm free!" said Tom to himself. "I'm a world traveler!"

He felt lonely. He felt very lonely. But he ate his crumb and his bit of bacon, and was brave.

The hills grew dark and vanished into the darkness. The stars shone out. The stars flew along with the train, always forward into the night. And Tom, watching at the window, called the stars his friends, because they traveled with him.

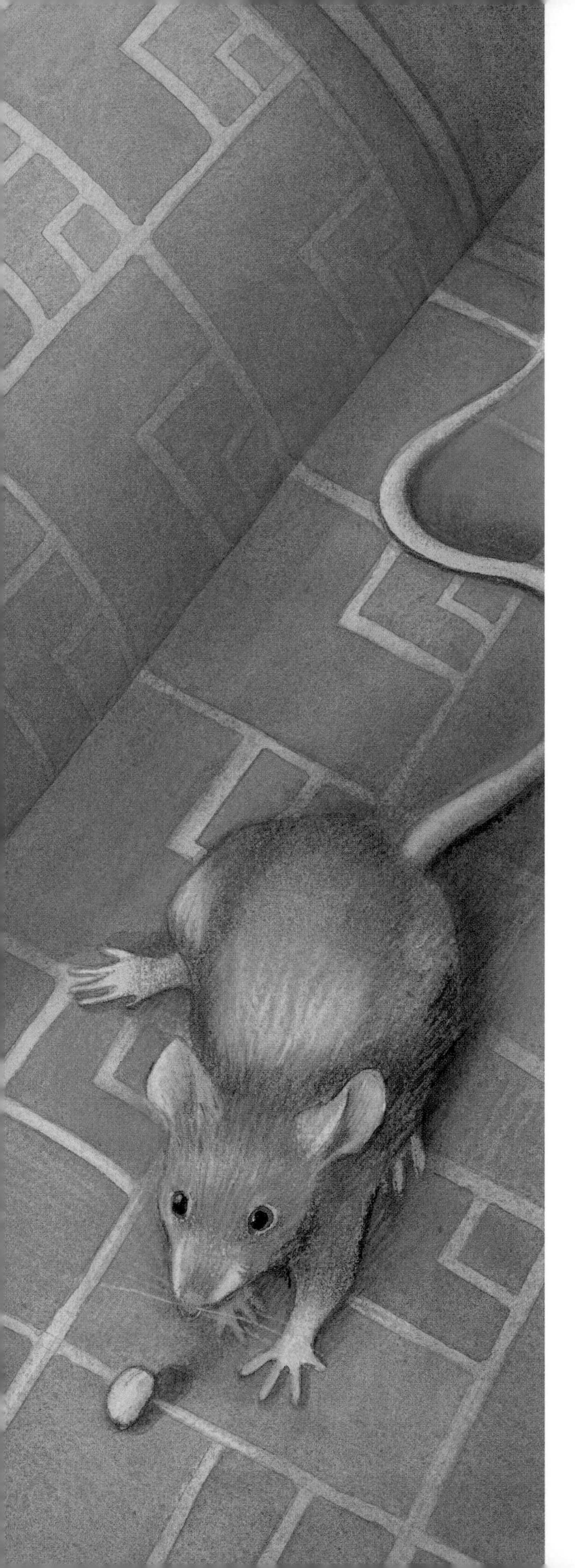

IN THE MORNING HE searched his new home very thoroughly. Its name was Roomette Nine. It had nothing to eat in it at all except one small, old peanut stuck deep in a seat corner. He ate the peanut and wondered where he could find more.

He was so busy searching Roomette Nine for the third time that he did not notice the train had stopped at a station.

When the porter came to the door, Tom had just time to whisk through the air vent into his closet and hide.

"There you are, Ms. Powers," said the porter's soft voice, and an even softer voice said, "Thank you, Mr. Morris." Tom cowered far back on the metal floor of the closet as suitcases were thumped about. The closet door was opened and a big red coat was hung up just over his head and a paper bag was shoved in, not leaving him much room on the floor.

He did not dare peep through the air vent until the train had started again and everything in Roomette Nine had been quiet for a long time.

An old woman sat on Tom's seat, at Tom's window, watching Tom's wide world fly by.

"She'll scream," Tom thought. "If she sees me she'll scream and stand on the seat and the porter will come with a broom."

People in his home station always screamed when they saw Tom or his family, and somebody always came running with a broom.

"Oh, well," Tom thought. "I can come out at night." And he turned his attention to the paper bag. Its smells were extremely interesting.

He had to investigate it more slowly and carefully than he would have liked, because the paper rattled and rustled. He nibbled a nice hole in the bottom, went in, and found five molasses cookies wrapped in waxed paper, some carrot sticks in a plastic bag, an apple, and a tin box of mints.

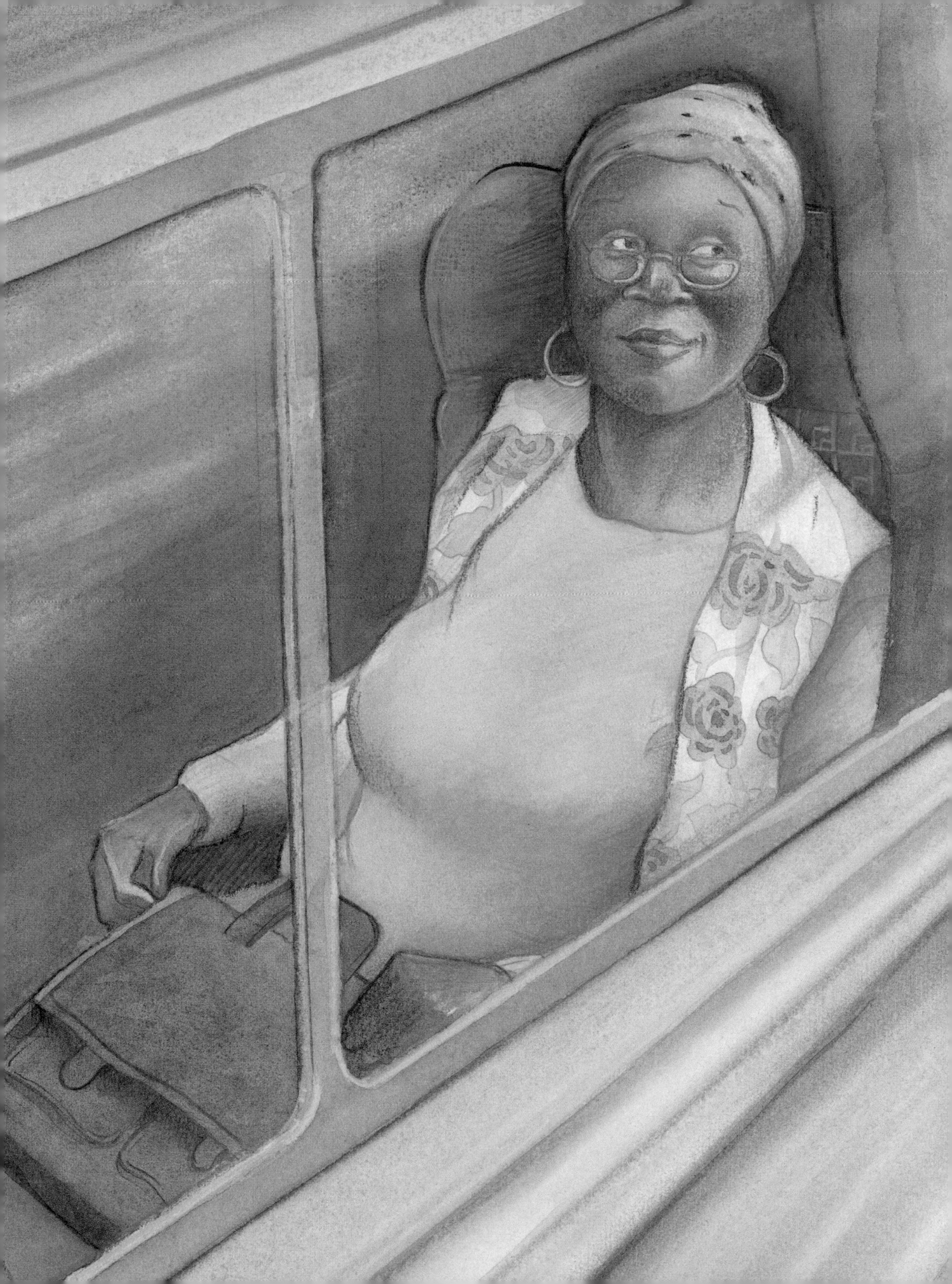

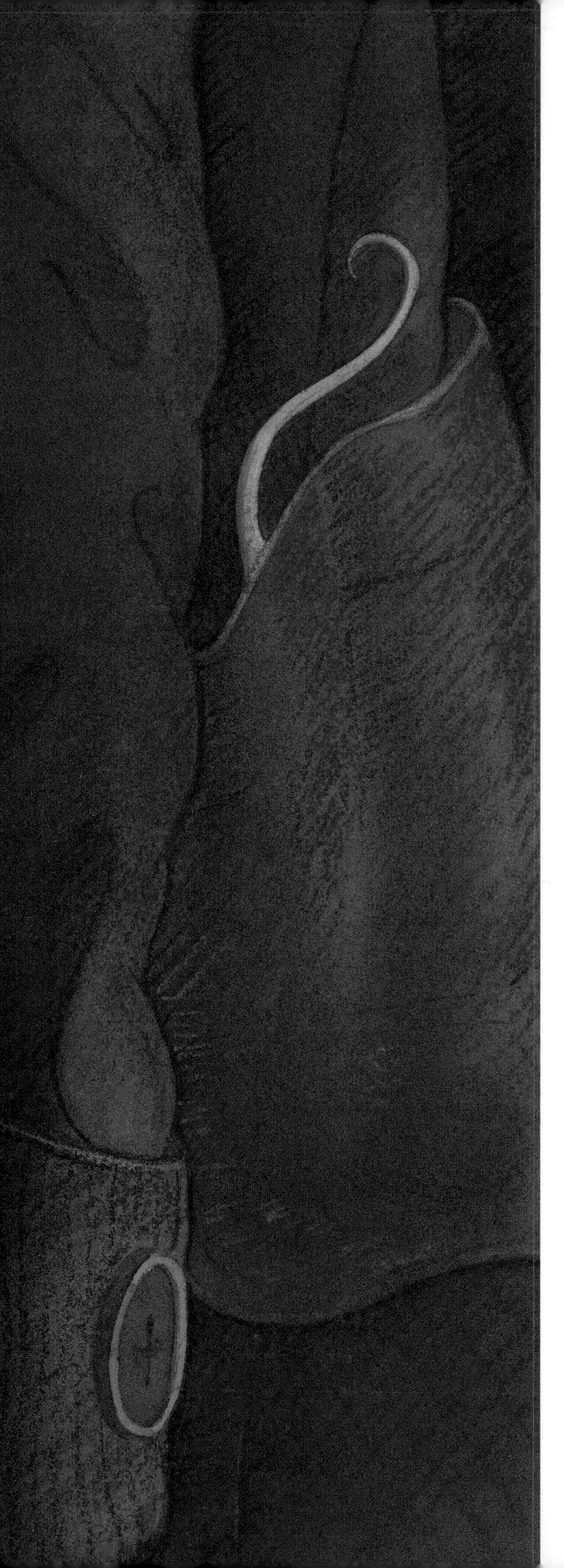

Tom removed a carrot stick and ate it very quietly, sitting on the closet floor. The soft red cloth of the coat swung just over his head. He climbed up it and found a lovely, deep, soft, warm pocket. He curled up there and fell fast asleep, rocked by the rhythm of the running train.

"First call for dinner!" said the loudspeaker in the corridor. Tom and the old woman both woke up with a start. The old woman took her handbag and left to go to the dining car. Tom removed a nice piece of molasses cookie from the bag and took it over to the window to eat, watching the wide world fly by in the twilight. When he heard the old woman talking to the porter, he whisked back into his closet.

Mr. Morris made a bed out of the two seats, with crisp sheets and a blue blanket. Ms. Powers got into the bed and read a book for quite a long time and then turned out the light.

After a while, when she was lying still and snoring a little sometimes, Tom crept out again. Very gently he walked over Ms. Powers to the window. There he sat and watched his friends the stars run with the running train. He wished they would talk to him, but they didn't.

He returned to the closet and fetched a carrot and another bit of cookie, being very quiet with the waxed paper. He ate his supper at the window, watching the moon rise over the far, dark hills.

"She's a very good cook," he thought, looking at the old woman asleep. "What a pity it is that she'd shriek and scream if she saw me here. How beautiful the moon is! I must dance."

Tom danced light as a little shadow over the blanket and over Ms. Powers, waving his tail and leaping in the air, making circles as round as the shining moon.

When his dance was done and dawn was in the sky, Tom returned to the warm coat pocket, with a quarter of a cookie for breakfast.

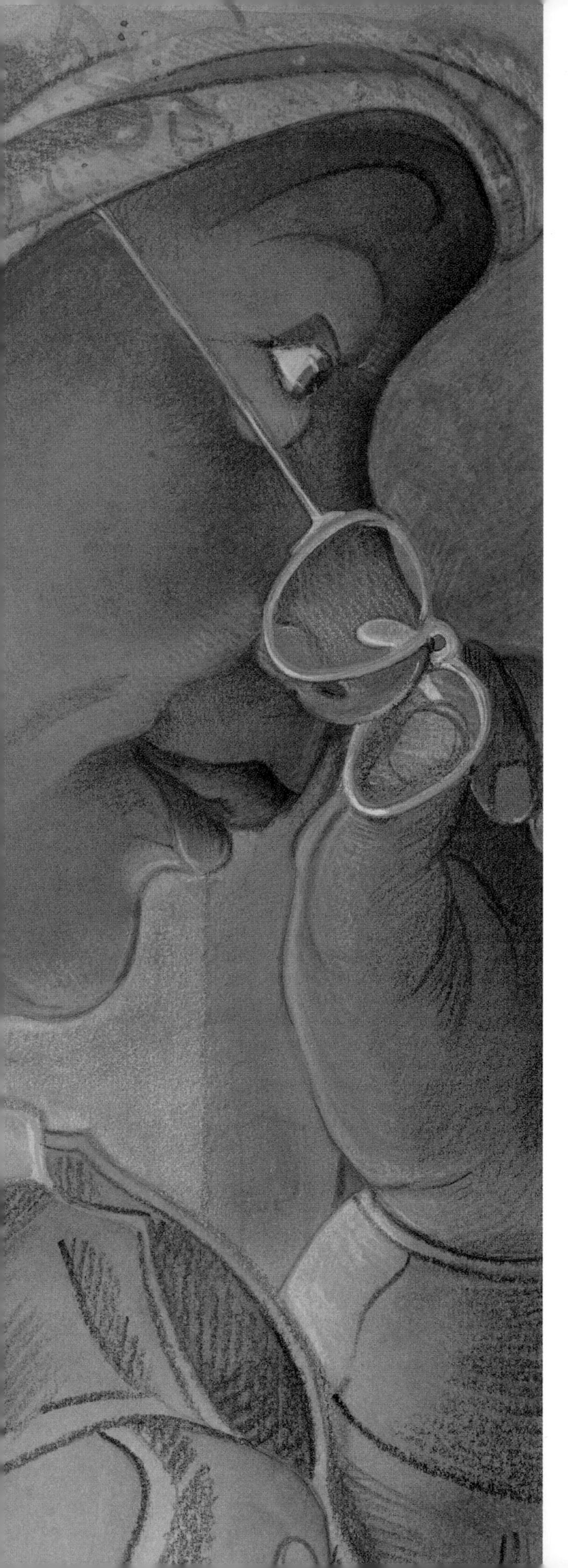

LATE IN THE MORNING the old woman put down her book and opened the closet door. She took out the paper bag. Tom heard her opening it and unwrapping waxed paper.

"Well," she said. "Well, well. My, my. Looks like we have a mouse."

She opened the closet door again quite suddenly—and there was Tom, on the edge of her coat pocket, staring her straight in the face.

She did not shriek or scream. She looked at Tom.

Tom, not knowing what else to do, looked at her.

"Mouse," she said, "you have been eating my cookies. You have been eating my carrots."

Tom could not deny it.

"Well," she said, "you'd better finish these two cookies, since you started on both of them. And you may have the carrots. Thank you for leaving me the apple and the mints." She put the carrots and the remains of the cookies on the closet floor and closed the door. Then she opened it again. Tom was still staring in amazement from her coat pocket.

"You keep that pocket tidy," she said. "No mess. No crumbs. You hear?"

Tom's whiskers shivered and his bright eyes shone.

"You dance beautifully," the old woman said, and shut the closet door.

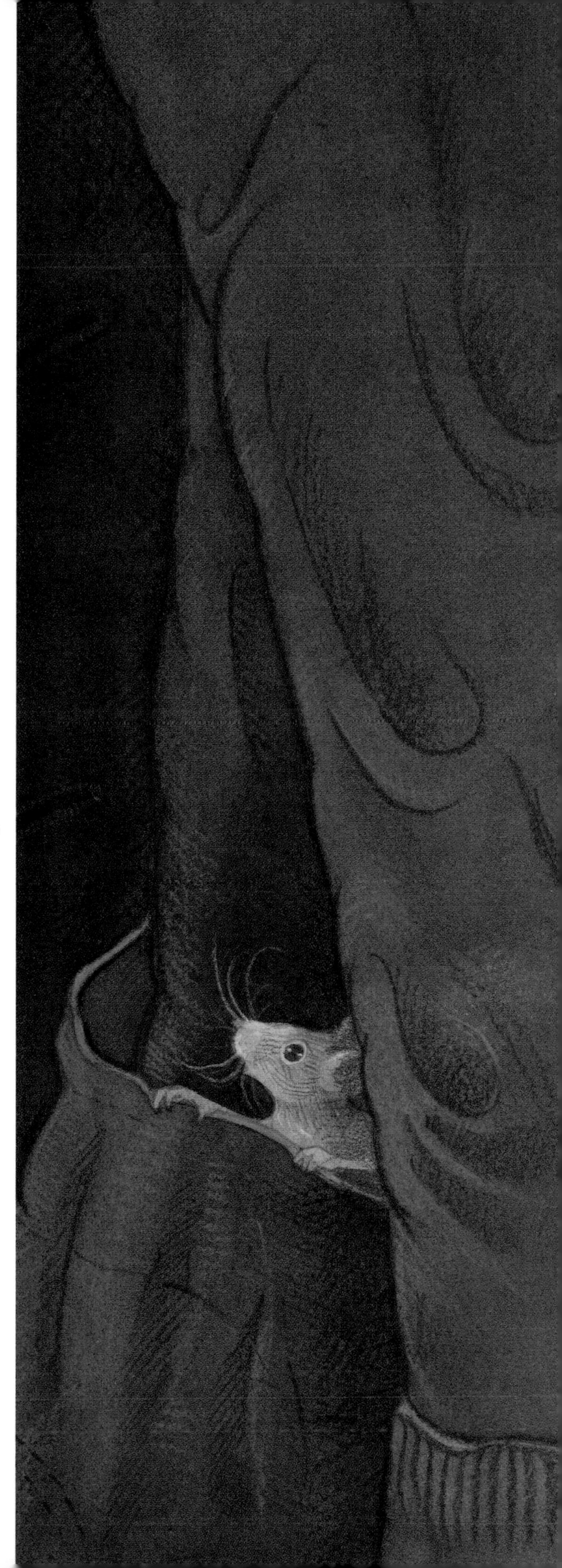

Tom spent the afternoon in his closet, thoughtfully eating cookies and trying not to make crumbs.

That night, when she came back from dinner in the dining car, Ms. Powers had a piece of cheese wrapped in a paper napkin. She put the napkin and the cheese down on the floor of the closet and shut the door again.

As she read her book, and Tom ate the cheese, he thought again, "Oh, what a wonderful cook she is!"

When Mr. Morris came to make up the bed for her, Ms. Powers asked him, "Do you ever have mice on trains?"

The young woman in Roomette Eight, across the corridor, was listening. She shrieked. "Mice! Ugh! There aren't any mice *here,* are there?"

"Well, they can be a pest," the porter said. "I don't like to find mice in the car, because when we do we have to send the car to the yards to be fumigated. You haven't seen any running around, have you, Ms. Powers?"

"Mice? Running around? What a notion!" said Ms. Powers. "My, my, just think, we'll be in Chicago tomorrow morning!"

"Sure will," said Mr. Morris. "Sleep well now."

"You sleep well, too," said Ms. Powers.

The instant she had shut the sliding door of Roomette Nine, she opened the door of the closet and spoke sternly to Tom, though she could not see him hiding in the back corner behind her coat.

"Mouse!" she said. "Did you hear that? They fumigate the cars! That means poison gas! To kill mice!"

Tom crouched shuddering in the darkest corner.

"The next passenger in this roomette, going back to San Francisco, might be like that silly girl across the corridor. She might see you and shriek and scream. Then Mr. Morris would have to report you!"

Tom had not a word to say.

"Now listen, mouse. If you're willing to trust me, I can get you out of here. I've got a nice shoe box at home, and no end of molasses cookies."

Tom was silent.

"Perhaps you like trains. Do you like traveling?" said Ms. Powers. She peered into the closet and saw Tom's nose and whiskers. "I suppose you could come with me," she said. "I travel a great deal on trains, and planes, too. And I get lonely. It would be nice to have a friend to travel with."

Tom's whiskers twitched.

“You’d have to stay hidden most of the time. But mice always do, don’t they? Well, think about it tonight, mouse. If you want to come, tomorrow morning, you know where my coat pocket is.”

And she closed the closet door.

That night, rain streaked the big window of Roomette Nine. There were no stars, no moon, only faint lights flying by in the darkness as the train ran forward. The old woman read her book, and turned out the light, and lay down.

Very quietly Tom squeezed through the air vent. Very lightly he walked across Ms. Powers to the window. He put his paws on the glass and looked out.

"It's all beautiful, isn't it?" the old woman said.

Tom's bright eyes shone like the raindrops on the glass as he watched the great darkness and the flying lights.

EARLY IN THE MORNING the train slowed down, coming in to Chicago.

"Going to ride with us again soon, Ms. Powers?" the porter asked her as he lifted her suitcase down.

"Next week, Mr. Morris. Back to San Francisco for a meeting about endangered species," she said. "And from there I'll fly to Tokyo for another meeting."

"They sure do keep you hopping!" said the porter. "Now, have you got everything?"

"Yes, I think so," said Ms. Powers, putting on her coat.

She did not put her hand into her left coat pocket, but she felt the outside of it very gently. Inside it was a tiny warm lump.

"Yes, thank you, everything is here!" she said to Mr. Morris. And to Tom she whispered, "Here you are, my friend!"

"Here I am!" thought Tom, curled up deep in the pocket. Despite all his efforts to be tidy it was quite littered with crumbs and little bits of carrot.

Ms. Powers walked down the steep, twisting stairs as the train pulled into the station. She stepped down onto the platform. "This is Chicago," she whispered.

"Chicago!" thought Tom, so excited that he stood up inside the pocket and gazed out over the edge.

Anybody could have seen his paws and his ears and his whiskers and his bright eyes, but nobody saw them, because nobody expected to see a mouse in an old woman's pocket.

Tom saw the big station, the big, busy city streets. He stared and stared as they got into a taxicab and the cars and people and the big buildings began to fly by.

Chicago and molasses cookies! Next week San Francisco and carrot sticks! And then an airplane flying to Tokyo! All the wide world, and all the cookies in it, and a friend!

"What a lucky mouse I am," thought Tom. "I'll dance for her every night."

And he did. He danced
all over the world for his friend.